The Mall from Outer Space

Look for these and other Apple Paperbacks in your local bookstore!

Haunted Island
  by Joan Lowery Nixon

Jamie and the Mystery Quilt
  by Vicki Berger Erwin

Ghosts Beneath Our Feet
  by Betty Ren Wright

The Haunting
  by Margaret Mahy

No Coins, Please
  by Gordon Korman

The Girl with the Silver Eyes
  by Vicki Berger Erwin

The Mystery at Peacock Place
  by M.F. Craig

The Mall from Outer Space

Outer Space

Todd Strasser

AN
APPLE
PAPERBACK

SCHOLASTIC INC.
New York Toronto London Auckland Sydney

ISBN 0-590-40319-2

12 11 10 9 8 7 6 5 4 3 2 1   7 8 9/8 0 1 2/9

Printed in the U.S.A.   28

First Scholastic printing, October 1987

To Steve, Brenda, Kim, and Josh

The Mall from Outer Space

1

I used to wonder sometimes what it would be like to have a normal little sister.

Like the day Sean Rabb and Dickie Fuller and I were over at the construction site for the new mall. Sean was on his skateboard, and Dickie and I had our freestyle bikes. We were freestyling all over this huge blacktop they'd laid down for the parking lot. It was really hot and sunny, and the asphalt was soft, which meant it didn't hurt as much if you fell.

For two weeks I'd been trying to learn to do a framestand — keeping the bike perfectly still with me standing on it. That day I finally got it.

"Radical move, man," said Sean, who had just moved here from someplace in California called Redondo Beach. He had a cast on his right arm because he'd broken his wrist when he fell off his bike two weeks ago.

"That's amazing," said Dickie, who comes from around here.

As you can probably imagine, I was feeling really proud. Sean has short, spiky blond hair and always wears sunglasses. He knows a lot about bikes and boards, and even has Mike Dominguez's autograph. He showed me how to do the framestand, but he never said I'd done a rad move until then.

"Stretch it out, dude," he said, smiling.

It wasn't easy. With both feet on the bike frame and my hands in the air for balance, I was struggling to keep from falling. But I was determined to hang in as long as I could.

Then Dickie said, "Hey, look, it's Nature Girl."

Clunk! My rad move was over. My bike banged to the ground, and I barely managed to land on my feet next to it. From the swamp on the other side of the parking lot, my sister Erin appeared, wearing yellow rubber boots, shorts, and a T-shirt. She was carrying a long-handled fishing net and a bucket.

"Who's that?" Sean asked.

"That's Dwight's little sister," Dickie said. "Nature Girl Osborn."

"What a trip," Sean said.

I'd heard my sister called worse things. She's ten

years old, a little under five feet tall, skinny, with long light-brown hair that's always in a ponytail. The boots she was wearing were my mother's. They were about three sizes too big on her. She clopped like an old horse as she ran toward us.

Finally she reached us and put the bucket down. She'd gotten green slime all over Mom's boots. Her legs and shorts were splattered with mud, but she didn't care. "Look what I caught!" she gasped, out of breath from running.

Sean and Dickie looked. I didn't have to. Whatever it was, I'd be seeing plenty of it soon enough.

"It's a turtle," Dickie said.

"*Emydoidea blandingi*," Erin corrected him.

"What?"

"Talk English, Erin," I said.

"It's a Blanding's turtle," Erin said. "Some people mistake it for a box turtle, but it's an aquatic species, not a land species. And it's not usually found around here."

My sister reached into the bucket and picked the turtle up. It made a hissing sound as it drew its head and legs into its shell. Erin pulled one of its legs out.

"See? The feet are webbed for swimming."

Sean and Dickie both nodded. Erin gently returned the turtle to the bucket. "I can't wait to

3

tell Mr. Duncan," she said. Mr. Duncan was Erin's favorite science teacher at school.

"But school's over for the summer," Dickie said.

"So?" Erin said. "I'll write him a letter. He's in New York this summer, doing research at the Bronx Zoo." She picked up the bucket and ran toward our house.

We watched her clop away. Then Dickie turned to me. He's kind of fat, with longish brown hair. His face turns red a lot. "She writes to her teacher during the summer?"

I shrugged. "At least once a week."

"What does she write about?"

"All the animals she finds."

"What's she gonna do with that turtle?" Sean asked.

"She'll watch it for a couple of weeks."

"Watch it?"

"Yeah. She'll watch it eat and swim," I said. "And she'll weigh it and make notes about it in her notebook. Then she'll let it go."

"Why does she make notes?" Dickie asked.

"So she'll be able to see how much it's grown the next time she catches it," I said.

"You mean there's things in that swamp she's already caught once?" Sean asked.

"Oh, yeah," I said. "She's caught some things three or four times."

Sean looked back at Erin. By now she was just a yellow and white dot clopping toward the houses across the road. "Far out," he said.

2

By the time I got home, the Blanding's turtle had joined the other residents of the Osborn Zoo. The zoo was about thirty feet long, and took up most of our back porch. It was long and narrow and had three rows of fish tanks on either side. On the shady side of the porch were the aquariums where the frogs, salamanders, turtles, and water snakes lived. On the sunny side were the terrariums where Erin kept insects, land snakes, box turtles, and toads.

Erin had turned her bucket upside down and was sitting on it, staring into a tank. On her lap was her notebook.

"The *Paratenodera sinensis* eggs are hatching," she whispered to me, as if talking louder might disturb them.

I looked into the tank and saw tiny little green things crawling out of something that looked like mattress stuffing. It didn't really bother me that Erin found stuff like that interesting. But something else was bothering me.

"It's bad enough that everyone around here thinks you're weird," I said. "But now that you're talking in that strange language, they're really gonna think you've flipped."

"That strange language just happens to be Latin," Erin said without taking her eyes off *Paratenodera sinensis*. "And that's how you say the correct scientific names."

"Well, do me a favor and save the scientific names for Mr. Duncan," I said.

"Why should I?" Erin asked.

"Because all my friends think you're totally abnormal," I said. "And I'm getting tired of trying to explain to them that you're only semitotally abnormal."

"Why bother?" Erin asked.

"Because you're my sister," I said. "And if you're abnormal, they're gonna start to think that I must be abnormal, too. It's called abnormal by association."

Erin turned and looked at me. She had that sly smile on her face. "But everyone knows *you're* normal, Dwight. It's perfectly normal to spend two whole weeks trying to stand on a bicycle."

That made me mad. Erin was an expert at twisting everything around. My parents said she was too smart for her own good. All I knew was she could really tick me off.

"Listen," I yelled at her. "It's a lot more normal for a guy my age to be doing that than it is for a girl your age to be crawling around in the swamp trying to catch things with Latin names."

"Every living thing has a Latin name," Erin said. "Even you. Do you want to know what your Latin name is?"

"No!" I shouted.

"Homo sapiens!" Erin shouted back.

"I am not!" I shouted back.

"Yes, you are," Erin yelled. "And so is Mom and so is Dad and so is every person on Earth."

"Okay, cut it out!"

Erin and I jumped. We were so busy screaming at each other that neither of us noticed my father stick his head out of the kitchen window.

"Erin said you, Mom, and I are *Homo sapiens,*" I told him.

My father smirked. "Listen, I don't care if she says we're guinea pigs. You two work out your own problems. Just don't shout."

"It's impossible to work out anything with her,"

I said. "The only things she cares about are her dumb animals."

"Well, you'll just have to work it out," my father said again. "But keep the noise down." Then he pulled his head back inside and closed the window. Sort of like a turtle pulling back into its shell.

"Look," I said to Erin. "Why don't you just stay away from me and my friends, okay? Stay in the swamp. Don't talk to us, and don't show us any animals with Latin names."

I know Erin heard me, but she didn't bother to reply. She was staring at *Paratenodera sinensis* like nothing else existed in the world.

3

After dinner that night I went back outside to practice some freestyle tricks on my bike. It was late June, and the days were long. It didn't get dark until almost nine o'clock. As I rode down the driveway, I noticed Erin lying on her stomach on the grass in the front lawn, looking through a magnifying glass. I knew she was looking at leafhoppers, those tiny bugs that live in the grass. She showed me some once. They're pretty cool-looking little guys with a lot of neat colors, but only Erin could watch them for hours.

Even though we'd had that fight before dinner, I felt kind of bad seeing her all by herself on the lawn. She was almost always doing things alone. She said she liked being by herself, but I didn't believe her.

I stopped in the driveway and practiced a side

glide. "What are you gonna do tomorrow?" I asked as I balanced on the bike.

Erin shrugged and kept looking at bugs.

"There's a girl who lives across the street from Dickie," I said. "I saw her today just hanging around by herself."

"Janice Pragers," Erin said.

"Maybe she's not doing anything tomorrow either," I said.

Erin didn't answer. When she didn't want to talk about something, she'd just tune you out like you didn't exist.

"Maybe you should call her," I said.

Erin still ignored me. It was no use. My sister was basically antisocial. I started to peddle out of the driveway, but suddenly Erin called me. "Dwight?"

I stopped my bike. "Yeah?"

"You know what a Dumpster is?" she asked.

It was a weird question, but, knowing Erin, I wasn't surprised. "You mean one of those big metal trash bins restaurants and stores use for garbage?"

"Is there any way that you could imagine a Dumpster flying?" Erin asked.

"Sure, if you had one of those big Huey helicopters like they use in the army."

"No, I mean flying by itself," Erin said.

"You mean leaving the ground and flying around?" I asked.

"Something like that," Erin said.

Now that was weird, even for Erin. I was really starting to worry about her. The kid was definitely spending too much time by herself. First it's flying Dumpsters, then little green men from Mars, and finally a one-way ticket to the funny farm.

"Hey," I said. "You want to come over to Dickie's with me tomorrow? We're gonna build a freestyle ramp."

"I thought you didn't want me to hang around with you and your friends," Erin said.

"I changed my mind."

Erin thought it over. "No, I'd rather go back to the swamp."

"Then, do me a favor," I said. "Don't say anything to Mom or Dad about flying Dumpsters, okay? We'll pretend it's our secret."

Erin sighed. "Sure, Dwight."

4

During the summer I never paid attention to what day it was. The only way I knew each week was over was because on Sundays Mom would do her aerobic exercises early in the morning before she went to church, and Dad would go for his once-a-week jog.

One morning I woke up because someone was shaking my arm. I opened my eyes and saw Erin in her pink pajamas. Her long, unbrushed hair was hanging over her shoulders. I wasn't real happy to see her.

"How come you woke me up?" I asked, rubbing my eyes. I felt like I could have slept another eight hours.

Erin brought her finger to her lips. "Shhh. Listen."

I listened. Downstairs I could hear the muffled

sounds of my parents talking and the clinking of coffee cups.

"So?" I said.

"It's Sunday," said Erin.

"No, it isn't," I said. "If it were Sunday, Mom would be doing her exercises, and Dad would be out jogging."

"That's just it," Erin whispered. "It is Sunday, and they're not doing that."

I listened again. There was no doubt about it. They weren't acting like it was Sunday.

"What do you think is going on?" I asked.

"You should sneak downstairs and find out," Erin said.

"Why me?" I asked.

"Because if it's something serious and they catch you, they'll feel better if you know and not me," Erin said.

It sounded like pretty strange logic to me, but now I was curious. I got out of bed and tiptoed down the stairs as quietly as I could. Then I stopped on the last step and listened.

"I don't know what we'll do," my father said in a grave voice.

"Let's not worry now," my mother said. "We'll just have to wait and see."

Whatever it was, it sounded serious. I wanted

to stay and listen, but a ball of paper hit me in the back of the head. I turned around and looked up the stairs. Erin waved at me to come back.

"What were they talking about?" she asked after I'd climbed the stairs.

"Can't tell, but it sounds serious," I said.

Erin thought for a moment. Then she said, "We shouldn't let them know we were listening. You should go downstairs the way you normally do."

"What do you mean, 'like I normally do'?" I asked.

"You know. Like a herd of wild elephants is chasing you."

"You really think you're smart," I said, although I knew she was right. As usual.

I went down the stairs and into the kitchen. Erin followed me. Our parents were sitting at the table. My father was wearing his red jogging suit, and my mother was wearing her exercise tights. They were both drinking coffee. The newspaper was folded up on the table.

"Morning, kids," Dad said.

"Uh, morning, Dad," I said. I looked around the kitchen to see if there was any sign of what was wrong. But everything looked normal. "How come you haven't gone jogging yet?"

Dad blinked. "You're right," he said, getting

up. "I was just about to go. See you later." He got up, kissed my mother on the cheek, and went out the back door.

"What do you kids want for breakfast?" Mom asked after he'd gone.

"I'll have — " I began to say, but Erin suddenly cut in.

"We'll make our own breakfast, Mom, so you can go exercise."

Mom smiled. "Why, that's very sweet of you. Okay, I'll leave you two alone. Just try not to make too much of a mess." She left the kitchen.

I turned to Erin. "Why'd you do that? I don't want to make breakfast."

Erin rolled her eyes at me like I was a dummy. "I wanted to get her out of the kitchen so we can figure out what's wrong," she whispered.

"How are we supposed to figure it out if they're not here?" I asked.

Erin started to chew on the skin next to her thumbnail. She did that when she was thinking really hard. "Well, they were wearing their exercise clothes. That means everything was still normal when they got dressed."

She looked around. "It must have been something they discovered when they came down for breakfast. . . . The newspaper!"

I looked at the paper, lying on the table. "What about it?"

"Look how it's folded," Erin said. "Usually it's spread out all over the place."

"So?"

"So I bet they came downstairs and started reading it like any normal Sunday," Erin said as she stepped toward the kitchen table. "But then they must have read something that upset them. And they don't want us to know, so they folded the paper back up as if they'd never read it in the first place."

It sounded to me like Erin's imagination was in overdrive. Anyway, I was starved. So while Erin opened the paper and started reading, I got myself a bowl and filled it with Cheerios.

A few minutes later, Erin whispered. "Here it is!"

"What?"

"Listen." Erin started reading. "The Galactic Mall Corporation yesterday announced the new tenants for their eighty-two-thousand-square-foot West Side Mall now under construction. . . ." She quickly read down the list of stores. "SoundWorld Records and Tapes."

"Another record store!" I said.

Erin nodded. She suddenly had an awful look

17

on her face. Almost like she was going to cry. Except she never cried.

"Hey, Erin," I said. "It's not that bad. I mean just because there's going to be another record store. . . ."

"It's not that," Erin said in a low voice.

"Then, what?" I asked.

Erin pointed to the last paragraph of the story:

The developers also announced that they would fill in the swamp adjacent to the new mall to make room for additional parking.

"They can't do that," Erin said. "That swamp is a home for millions of living things. They can't destroy it."

"I don't know, Erin," I said. "The Galactic Mall Corporation sounds like a pretty big company. I have a feeling they can do anything they please."

But my sister shook her head. "They don't understand. If they knew what they were doing, I'm sure they'd change their minds." She folded the newspaper and stood up.

"What are you going to do?" I asked.

"I'm going to write a letter to the president of the Galactic Mall Corporation," Erin said.

5

Erin went to write her letter to the president of the Galactic Mall Corporation, and I went over to Sean's. Sean and his mother had moved into a ranch house in one of the new developments in town. We were going to build a plywood freestyle ramp in his driveway. Some of the houses in the development weren't finished yet, and Sean had gathered up a bunch of used two-by-fours, plywood sheets, and nails left behind by the construction workers. We were following the instructions on how to build the ramp from an old copy of *Freestylin'* magazine.

We worked most of the morning on the frame for the ramp. Sean had a couple of hammers and a saw. He pulled old nails out of the wood, and then I used a pliers to straighten them so they could be used again. Dickie was sawing. It was hard work, and his face got red. After a while we took a break, and Sean got us some sodas from his house.

"What does your dad do back in California?" Dickie asked Sean while we sat and drank the sodas.

"He does helicopter traffic reports," Sean said.

"You mean he flies around in a helicopter?" Dickie asked.

"Yeah."

"That's really cool," Dickie said. "Did he ever let you fly it?"

"Well, I'm not supposed to tell anyone," Sean said. "But I guess it doesn't matter here. Yeah, he showed me how to fly it."

"Is it hard?" I asked.

Sean shook his head. "I was pretty scared at first, but it was easy."

"I wish I could fly a helicopter," Dickie said.

"What does your father do?" Sean asked him.

"He just fixes vending machines and video games," Dickie said.

"What about your father?" Sean asked me. We'd finished our sodas and started hammering the two-by-fours together.

"He has a record store in town," I said. "Osborn's."

"You must get a lot of records," Sean said.

"Yeah, but I don't like music that much," I said. "My father's a real music nut. That's why he has the store. Only I don't know how much longer he's gonna have it."

"How come?" Sean asked.

"They're putting a big record store in that new mall," I said.

"Yeah," Dickie said. "I can't wait till they finish that mall. It's gonna be great."

"Well, it's not gonna be great for my father," I said. "It's gonna hurt the business at his store. A couple of years ago they opened that mall on the east side of town, and it took away all his business from the people who lived there. Now he's going to lose a lot of customers from the west side of town, too."

"He'll still have the north and south sides of town," Dickie said with a grin. He was making a joke, since there was nothing on the north side of town except a big reservoir. And the south side of town was mostly old factories and junkyards.

"Doesn't your father have loyal customers who'll come to his store anyway?" Sean asked.

"Sure, he's got some," I said. "But a lot of people will go to the mall because it'll be new and different. It'll be a lot easier to park cars there than it is in town. And they'll have all kinds of food places and games like they have at all the other malls. Wouldn't you rather go there?"

Sean nodded.

"I heard my parents talking this morning," I said. "It sounded like they were worried that this new mall could put my father out of business."

"What would happen then?" Dickie asked.

"I don't know," I said. "I guess he'd have to get another job."

"That's not so bad," Dickie said.

"Except we might have to move," I said.

"Why?"

"Because his new job might be in another town," I said. "Or even in another state. Or, he might get a job around here, but maybe the salary wouldn't be so good. Then we'd have to move to a cheaper place to live."

"Man, I can relate to that," Sean said. "Before my parents got divorced, we lived in a really nice house with a swimming pool and everything. We always had cool stuff to eat, and we'd go out a lot. After the divorce my mother had to move here, and we're on a really tight budget. Like all she makes to eat these days is stuff with cheese melted on it. Melted cheese sandwiches, melted cheese on toast, tomatoes and melted cheese, cauliflower with melted cheese. . . . I never knew there were so many things you could melt cheese on until my parents got divorced."

"I don't even like cheese," Dickie said.

"Well, if your parents get divorced, watch out," Sean said. "You could be eating a lot of it."

Dickie looked back at me. "What are you going to do?"

I shrugged. "I don't know. Erin's writing a letter to the president of the company that's building the mall."

"That's gonna do a lot of good," Dickie said with a laugh.

"She's really writing about the swamp," I said. "She read in the paper this morning that they plan to pave it over."

"That would be great," Dickie said. "My mom says she's always getting bitten by the mosquitoes from that place. And my old man says the raccoons get into everyone's garbage."

"Well, you know how Erin feels about it," I said. "She spends a lot of time there."

Dickie got up and started walking like Frankenstein. "The creature from the swamp," he said. "It walks, it talks, it's in all G and T classes."

"G and T?" Sean said.

"It means geeks and twerps," Dickie said.

"It stands for gifted and talented," I said. "It's for smart kids."

"Gnomes and toads," said Dickie.

"Your sister's a real brain?" Sean asked.

"Yeah. She's ten, but she skipped a grade, so next year she'll be in sixth," I said. "She's in all G and T classes except science."

"Doesn't she like science?" Sean asked.

"Sure, it's her best subject," I said. "The trouble is, she took sixth-grade G and T science last year. They don't know what to do with her next year."

"Didn't you once say her IQ was something like one hundred and sixty?" Dickie said.

"One sixty-three," I said.

"That's genius," Dickie said. "But if being a genius means you have to be as weird as Erin, I'm glad I'm not one."

"She's not weird," I said. "She's just into different things than us. To her, freestyling is weird."

"Maybe," Dickie said. "But I'll bet you anything there are a lot more kids who freestyle than there are who hang around in swamps catching turtles."

"My mother used to belong to this group called the Sierra Club," Sean said. "They were really into swamps and stuff, and they were always protesting against companies that wanted to pave over places where animals lived."

"I think it'll be good if they pave over the swamp," Dickie said. "Then she'll have to get into more normal stuff."

"She's not abnormal," I said, getting angry.

"Okay, okay," Dickie said. "She's normal. But just a little weird."

6

We had just finished the ramp frame when out of the corner of my eye I noticed someone racing up the street on a bike. It was Erin on her old red Schwinn. It had a wire basket on the front and balloon tires. She stopped on the street and waved to me.

"Oh, Dwight, it's Nature Girl," Dickie sang.

"What do you want?" I called to her.

"Come here, I need to talk to you," Erin yelled.

"You come here," I said.

But Erin shook her head.

"Nature Girl must have a secret," Dickie said. "I bet she's found something new in the swamp, and she doesn't want anyone to know about it. Maybe it's her new boyfriend. The Creature from the Black Lagoon."

"Please, Dwight," Erin said.

"Please, Dwight, please!" Dickie mimicked her.

I knew Dickie would keep making fun of her, so I went down the driveway and out to where Erin was waiting in the street. "What is it?"

"I have to show you something."

"But I'm working on the ramp," I said.

"This is important," Erin said.

"Tell me what it is."

"You have to see for yourself," Erin said.

"Forget it," I said. "I want to stay here with my friends."

"Dwight, if you don't come with me right now, I'm going to hop around the street like a frog and make croaking noises in Latin."

I glanced back at Dickie and Sean. "Go ahead. I don't care."

Erin got off her bike and started to squat. I knew Dickie would love it. I could just imagine him telling everyone he knew what a totally abnormal sister I had.

"Okay, stop," I said. "You win."

Erin smiled and got back on her bike. I went back up the driveway to get my bike.

"Going somewhere?" Sean asked.

"Uh, yeah," I said, getting on my bike.

"Have fun with Nature Girl." Dickie grinned.

I rode down the driveway and started riding with my sister. "Where are we going?" I asked.

"To the swamp."

We rode to the edge of the swamp and stopped. A lot of big trees grew in there, and it always looked dark, even during the day. It was filled with all kinds of bushes and reeds and old tree trunks with moss and vines hanging off them. Frankly, the place gave me the creeps.

Erin got off her bike and started to walk in, but I stayed by the edge. She stopped and looked at me. "Come on."

"Forget it, Erin," I said. "I'm not interested in looking at animals."

"I'm not going to show you animals," Erin said. "This is important."

"Then, tell me what it is," I said.

"I can't," Erin said. "You won't believe me. You'll have to see for yourself."

I shook my head. "No way."

"Please, Dwight," Erin said. "I really mean it. You have to come see."

"Why?"

"Because I'm going to show you something no one else in the whole world has ever seen," Erin said. She turned and started into the swamp. I sighed and watched her take the first few steps into the mud. I knew I was going to follow her. Of course, this *would* be the day I was wearing my favorite sneakers.

A few minutes later we were deep in the swamp. Erin seemed to know where to go to stay away from the really sticky, gooey mud. But my sneakers were caked anyway, and the water had soaked through to my socks. Mosquitoes were buzzing around my head, and I'd been bitten twice so far.

"This better be good," I said.

Erin didn't say anything.

Besides the buzzing of the mosquitoes and the plopping sounds our sneakers made as we trudged through the mud, the swamp was almost perfectly quiet. It was kind of eerie, but nice, too. I could almost see why the animals liked to live there. No one bothered them. Except Erin, of course.

Ahead of me, Erin stopped next to a tree and looked up. Above in the branches I could just see a small wooden platform hidden in the leaves.

"What's that?" I asked.

"An observation blind," Erin said. "I built it so I could watch and not be seen. I've got four of them around the swamp."

We walked a little farther, and then Erin put her finger to her lips and pointed through the trees and bushes. I crouched down next to her and looked. About twenty feet ahead of us was a clearing. The brush had been cleared away, and it looked like there was sand on the ground. In the middle of the clearing was something big and green. Erin crept closer, and I followed. As I got closer, I saw what it was.

"A Dumpster?" I whispered.

Erin nodded.

We stopped at the trees at the edge of the clearing. The Dumpster sat on the sand in front of us. On the sides the name GALACTIC HAULERS, LTD. had been stenciled in white letters. I thought it sounded like a cool name for a garbage truck company. But I was still a little annoyed.

"This is what you wanted to show me?" I whispered.

"Yes."

"I thought you said it was something no one had ever seen before," I said. "I've seen a million Dumpsters."

"In the middle of a swamp?"

"So? Someone must have dragged it in here," I said.

"How?"

She had a point. The clearing was surrounded by a thick growth of trees. There was no way anyone could have dragged a Dumpster through them.

"How do you think it got here?" I asked.

Erin gave me a long, cool look. "It landed here," she said at last.

I gave her a long, skeptical look in return.

"Is there any other way it could have gotten here?" Erin asked.

I looked around again. There really wasn't.

"It could have been dropped by helicopter," I said.

"It wasn't," Erin said.

"How do you know?"

Erin looked at me again. "I saw it."

"What did you see?" I asked.

"I saw it land."

"What!?"

"I was up in the blind watching a family of raccoons when it just came out of the sky and landed there."

"Erin, you've really gone nuts this time."

My sister sighed. "Listen, Dwight. You know how I was going to write a letter to the president of the Galactic Mall Corporation? Well, I looked in the phone book, and there is no Galactic Mall Corporation. So I called Information, and they had no listing. So then I went over to the library and asked the librarian to look it up for me. She went through every business book and magazine they had and still no listing."

"So what's the point?"

"As far as I can tell, no one has ever heard of the Galactic Mall Corporation. And two days ago I saw that Dumpster drop out of the sky and land there. Somehow I have a feeling the two things are related."

I had two choices. I could decide that Erin was crazy, or I could take a closer look at the Dumpster. I decided to take a closer look.

"Be careful," Erin said.

"You think it could be dangerous?" I asked.

"I don't know."

I stepped out from behind the trees and walked slowly up to the Dumpster. It was a big one. The sides were over my head. It looked like any other Dumpster, except that it wasn't banged up and dented like most. I walked around it once and didn't see anything unusual. But the top was open.

I decided to climb up and take a look inside.

"What are you doing?" Erin gasped from the trees.

"Just taking a look," I said, grabbing onto the side of the Dumpster. "Don't worry."

I pulled myself up and looked in. Instantly I knew this was no ordinary Dumpster. The inside was unreal. It looked more like an airplane cockpit than a garbage can. There were dials and meters and lots of switches. . . .

"*Dwight!*" Erin whispered urgently.

I quickly looked back toward the trees. "What?"

"Listen."

I held perfectly still for a second. In the distance I could hear something. *Ker-plop, ker-plop, ker-plop.* Someone was walking through the swamp. It sounded like they were getting closer. I jumped down off the Dumpster and ran back to the trees. Erin was on her stomach, watching.

"Come on, let's get out of here," I whispered.

"No, I want to see."

"We'll get caught," I said.

"Not if you get down and stay quiet," Erin said. "Besides, we haven't done anything wrong."

"Listen," I whispered. "If that thing really landed here, it may not matter whether we've done anything wrong."

Erin didn't answer. I knew I wasn't going to get her to leave. She gave new meaning to the word *stubborn*.

We waited about a minute and then we saw someone come through the woods on the other side of the Dumpster. He was wearing a blue security guard's uniform with a big orange and red patch on the shoulder that said GALACTIC SECURITY CO. In one hand he twirled a long wooden nightstick. He had a mustache and a big belly that hung over the belt of his pants.

He came out into the clearing and strolled toward the Dumpster. He didn't look surprised to find it there. He tapped it once with the nightstick and then stuck his head over the side and looked in. Then he walked a few feet away and knelt down as if he were looking at something in the sand.

"What's he doing?" Erin whispered.

"Can't see," I whispered back.

After a few seconds the security guard stood up. He took a white handkerchief out of his pocket and dabbed his forehead. Then he headed back into the swamp.

When he was out of sight, Erin stood up. "Come on," she said in a low voice.

I got up, expecting her to head back out of the swamp, but instead she started toward the clearing.

"Where are you going?" I asked.

"I want to see what he was looking at," Erin said.

"Are you crazy? What if he comes back?"

"We'll be quiet," Erin said.

7

What choice did I have? I couldn't talk her out of it, and I wasn't going to leave her there alone. Erin walked quietly into the clearing and knelt down in the sand where the guard had knelt.

"Dwight, look at this."

I knelt down next to her. As I watched, Erin brushed some of the sand away. Under it was a long metal hinge. She kept brushing sand away until we could see the outline of a pair of gray metal doors.

"What the . . . ?"

Erin brushed some more sand away. "There's no doorknob," she said.

"Where do you think it goes?" I asked.

"Don't know," Erin said. She reached down and touched the door. "Whatever's down there is cold."

I pressed my fingers against the metal. It felt

very cool. "Maybe it's a freezer or something."

"In the middle of the swamp?" Erin asked, getting up. She looked in the direction the guard had gone and then started to cross the sandy clearing.

"Where are you going?" I asked.

"I want to see where that guard goes," she said, and started through the trees. I followed, telling myself I was crazy.

We couldn't see him. Erin must have been following his footsteps in the mud.

"This feels like a real ambush setup to me," I whispered behind her, ducking the branches.

"You watch too much TV," Erin whispered back.

"Maybe this is TV," I said.

Erin looked back at me for a second. "What are you talking about?"

"Well, where else would you find a Dumpster full of electronic equipment in the middle of the swamp?" I asked.

"This isn't TV," Erin said.

"How can you be so sure?" I asked.

"Because we've been in it for almost half an hour and there hasn't been a single commercial," she said.

We followed the guard's trail to the edge of the swamp and then stopped. Ahead of us we could see the guard walking out through the high grass toward the new mall. I thought Erin would want to follow him, but I guess she knew it would be too easy to be seen. Instead we turned around and headed back through the swamp.

"I bet he's a security guard for the mall," Erin said later as we rode home on our bikes. "So that no one steals the building equipment or materials."

"Maybe," I said.

Erin rode with one hand and started biting the skin next to her thumbnail on the other. "And he knows about that Dumpster."

"And the door," I said.

"Did you notice the name of the company on his shirt?"

"The Galactic Security Company."

"Isn't that strange?" Erin asked. "The mall is being built by the Galactic Mall Corporation. The Dumpster belongs to Galactic Haulers, Ltd., and the security guard works for Galactic Security."

"Maybe it's a conglomerate."

"If it is, it would have to be a big company," Erin said. "But no one's ever heard of it."

We rode past Patton Field, a junky old park with a baseball diamond and a couple of old basketball hoops, and then down the street toward our community. The sun was still pretty high in the sky, but it was probably close to dinnertime. Too late to go back to Sean's. If Dickie, Sean, and I worked all day tomorrow, we'd probably have the ramp finished in time to try a few tricks. I wondered what Erin was thinking about, but I didn't have to wonder for long.

"I'm going to the mall tomorrow," she said. "Someone there will know how I can get to talk to the president of the company."

"Uh, I don't think that's such a good idea," I said.

"Why?"

"Because he's probably a pretty important person," I said. "What makes you think he has time to talk to ten-year-old girls."

"I can't let them pave over the swamp," Erin said. "And maybe I could talk to him about the record store, too."

I had to laugh. "Erin, they're not going to listen to you."

"How do you know? Remember that girl who wrote to the leader of the Soviet Union? They flew her all the way to Russia, and then she went on TV. They listened to her."

"Yes, but this is different," I said.

"Why?" Erin asked.

"I don't know why," I said, "but it just is."

"Well, I have to try," Erin said.

"But what if it's some kind of secret?" I said. "I mean, why else would they have a Dumpster like that? Maybe there's some kind of secret military operation behind it. Maybe they're spies or something."

"Building a mall?"

"Look, I don't know what's going on, and neither do you," I said. "But we both saw that Dumpster. Why would a normal company have something like that?"

"I don't know," Erin said. "Maybe I'll find out tomorrow."

"You know, you could really get into trouble," I said.

"If it means saving the swamp, then I don't care," Erin said. "Besides, they don't put ten-year-old girls in jail."

8

The next morning Mom knocked on my door. "Phone for you, Dwight." Then she went back downstairs.

I went downstairs and found the receiver lying on the kitchen table. From the den I could hear the sound of my mother's exercise record and Mom grunting along with it. I picked up the phone. "Hello?"

"Hey, dude." It was Sean.

"Hi."

"You gonna come over and help us finish the ramp today?" Sean asked.

"You bet."

"We need a Phillips-head screwdriver," Sean said. "Think you have one?"

"I could check," I said.

"Okay, see you later."

"Right."

After I hung up I went into the den. Mom was lying on her back on the floor. Twice a day she did forty minutes of aerobic exercises. Her legs were in the air above her, and she was holding a rubber kickball between her knees. She was doing crunches, which are like sit-ups. While the music played, a voice on the record counted out the number of crunches she was supposed to do. Mom grunted with each crunch.

"Thirty-eight," said the record.

"Unh," Mom grunted.

"Thirty-nine."

"Unh."

"Forty."

"Unh."

"Mom, does Dad have a Phillips-head screwdriver?" I asked.

"Forty-one," said the record.

"Unh," Mom grunted. "He might."

"You think it would be in the garage?" I asked.

"Forty-two," said the record.

"Unh. Try his workroom," said Mom.

"You think he'd mind if I took it?" I asked.

"Forty-three," said the record.

"Unh. Just make sure you put it back," said Mom.

"I will," I said.

I went downstairs into my father's workroom and found a Phillips-head screwdriver. Then I went up to the kitchen to have some breakfast before I went over to Sean's. I was just about finished with my cereal when Erin came in wearing a white dress with pink flowers on it.

"Are you feeling okay?" I asked. I also noticed that she'd brushed her hair and put a pink ribbon in it.

"Yes."

"Why are you all dressed up?"

"Well, if the president of the Galactic Mall Corporation is as important as you say he is, shouldn't I wear a dress?" Erin asked.

It was hard to believe that my sister could be so smart about some things and so dumb about others. "The president of the company isn't going to be at the mall," I said. "They haven't even finished building it yet. The president probably works in some office building in a city a thousand miles from here."

"But somebody has to be in charge of building the mall," Erin said. "And whoever it is, I want to make a good impression."

Just then Mom came in from the den. She had a

white towel around her neck, and her face was red and sweaty from exercising.

"Why, Erin, don't you look nice," she said as she opened the refrigerator and took out a bottle of club soda. "Is someone having a party today?"

My sister started biting the skin next to her thumbnail. "Yes. Janice Pragers is."

"Isn't it a little early in the day?" Mom asked.

"It's a brunch party," Erin quickly answered.

"Oh. How sophisticated," Mom said with a smile. "Do you want me to give you a ride over there?"

"Uh . . ." Erin glanced quickly at me.

"It's okay, Mom," I said. "I'll ride her on my bike. I'm going to Dickie's, and Janice lives right across the street."

Mom poured some club soda into a glass and gulped it down. "That's very nice of you, Dwight. I'm going to go upstairs and take a shower. Have a good time, Erin, and call me if you need a ride home after the party."

"I will, Mom."

We watched her leave the kitchen. Then I looked at Erin.

"A *brunch* party?" I whispered.

"I had to make up something," Erin whispered back.

"So what are you going to do now?" I asked.

"I'll go to the mall," she said.

"You can't just walk," I said. "Mom thinks you're going with me. What if she looks out the window and sees you?"

"Okay. Then you can give me a ride."

9

That's how I wound up giving Erin a ride to the mall. She sat on the handlebars of my bike, and I pedaled.

It looked busy when we got there. There were construction workers everywhere. Trucks owned by Galactic Construction, Ltd., were unloading big piles of pipe and steel beams. A tall red crane was lifting loads of long metal rods off a flatbed truck. The mall itself was still just a maze of concrete walls and metal supports, but at the rate everyone was working it wouldn't be long before it was completed.

I stopped in the parking lot, and Erin got off the bike. Near us a woman in construction clothes was pushing a machine that painted the white stripes between the parking spaces. She was wearing red coveralls and had a red bandanna on her forehead. It wasn't that hot out, but the bandanna was dark with sweat.

"Excuse me," Erin said.

The woman must have been concentrating on her job because she didn't even notice my sister.

"Excuse me," Erin said a little louder.

The woman still didn't hear her.

"I said excuse me!" Erin shouted.

The woman looked up at her and blinked. Then she looked at me. Then she went right back to work painting the lines.

"Maybe she's deaf," I said.

"Either that or she's really weird," Erin said.

About fifty feet away another worker was standing behind a tripod, looking through an instrument that resembled a little telescope. He was also wearing red coveralls and had big sweat stains under his arms. Erin walked over to him, and I followed.

"Excuse me," Erin said.

The man ignored her, just like the woman had. This time Erin didn't even bother to yell. She just raised her hand so that it blocked the instrument's view. The man behind the tripod looked up and frowned.

"I'm sorry I did that," Erin said, taking her

hand away. "But I just wanted to get your attention."

But the man ignored her and looked through the instrument again. Erin put her hand over it again. This time she didn't take it away when the man looked up.

"Could you tell me why you're ignoring me?" Erin said.

The man said nothing. He just reached toward Erin's hand and moved it out of the way.

Erin backed slowly toward me.

"There's something really strange going on," she said.

"Maybe they're just superbusy," I said.

"No way, Dwight," Erin said. "These people are different."

"What do you mean?" I asked.

"Didn't you see the way he moved my hand?" she asked. "Like it was just a thing. It could have been a piece of dirt or a bug. I could see it in their eyes. They have no idea what we are."

"You're crazy," I said. "Look." I got on my bike and rode in front of the tripod. Then I did a wheelstand so that I blocked the man's view.

For a second the man did nothing. Then he picked up the tripod and moved it to his left so

47

that he had a clear view. I moved over and did another wheelstand. He moved the tripod again.

"Hey, mister," I said. "Why don't you just tell me to get lost."

The man didn't answer. It was like he didn't know I was there.

"See?" Erin said.

"Yeah," I said, backing away on my bike.

"Isn't it weird?" Erin asked.

"Yeah, it's weird. And I think it's time we left."

"Why?"

"Because these people give me the creeps," I said. "There must be something totally bizarre going on around here, and I'd just as soon not be part of it."

"Wait, Dwight."

"Why?" I asked.

"Because if they don't know what we are, then they probably won't bother us," Erin said. "Let's just look around for a second."

"Okay, but just for a second," I said. I don't know why I agreed. I guess I was a little curious myself. Erin got back on my bike, and we rode around the construction site, staying clear of anything that looked dangerous. We passed big cement mixers and dozens of workers pouring cement for foundations. We passed backhoes and bulldozers. It seemed like we could have gone anywhere we wanted and no one would have stopped us.

"Let's go over there," Erin said, pointing at a part of the mall where no one was working.

I rode over. Up close we could see the rectangular concrete foundations where the basement of each store would go. Thick metal rods stuck out of the concrete walls. The whole place had that fresh concrete smell. Like a new sidewalk.

Erin got off the bike.

"Hey, where are you going?" I asked.

"I just want to look," Erin said.

"You shouldn't go in there," I said. But it was too late. Erin had already gone into the mall.

I got off the bike and jogged to catch up to her. Erin was walking down the middle of the mall, where the long corridor between the rows of stores would be.

"Erin, this is really a mistake," I said.

"No one's going to bother us," she said.

"Listen, it's one thing to just ride around the construction site," I said, "but to go in here is wrong. I mean, it's trespassing."

"I didn't see any signs, did you?" Erin said.

"That's not the point," I said.

Before Erin could answer, someone else spoke.

"You two! What are you doing?"

I jumped around just as a man in a brown suit caught up to us. He had short brown hair and looked a little like the man who came to our house once a year and sold my father insurance. Pinned to his jacket was a small blue plate that said GA-LACTIC PERSONNEL. He was carrying a clipboard filled with papers.

"Don't move," he said. He looked at us closely. "You could be loiterers, but I think you're sample shoppers." He flipped through the pages on the clipboard. "You're not supposed to be here until tomorrow." The man turned the clipboard around and showed it to us. "See?"

Erin and I looked at the clipboard. There were things written on it, but it was in a kind of writing I'd never seen before. I raised my eyebrows at Erin, trying to tell her to get ready to run.

The man took out a handkerchief and patted his forehead. I noticed that he had very pale skin, as if he had never been out in the sun. "How did you get here?" he asked.

I glanced at my sister. It was definitely time to run. But Erin stood still.

"Galactic Haulers," she said.

The man nodded. "Yes, of course. Stupid question. The correct question is: Why are you here?"

My heart started to pound. I was sure he was going to have us arrested for trespassing.

"We're sample shoppers," Erin answered.

"Yes, obviously you're sample shoppers," the man said. "You Betas are impossible to talk to." He thought for a moment. "All right. This is the actual question: Why are you here today instead of tomorrow?"

I was certain he was going to nail us now. But Erin just said, "I don't know."

"Hmmm," the man mumbled. "Right. Nobody tells Betas anything, and even if they did, you probably wouldn't understand anyway."

The man started looking through the pages again. Erin glanced at me and winked. The man looked at us again.

"Do you have any special instructions, requisitions, or bills of lading?"

Erin shook her head.

The man nodded. "Typical. Utterly typical. Okay. Listen carefully. You have to come back tomorrow. The sample shopper orientation program will begin at ten A.M. Understand?"

Erin nodded.

"And you shouldn't be out here," the personnel

man said. "Go back into the swamp, and tomorrow morning use the swamp entrance. You know where that is?"

Erin nodded again.

"All right. Your manager will meet you there in the morning. Now go."

Erin and I turned and headed toward the swamp. I figured I could double back later and get my bike.

"I can't believe you fooled that guy," I said. "I was sure he was going to nail us."

Erin didn't answer.

"Hey, what is it?" I asked.

"What do you think a Beta is, Dwight?" she asked.

"I don't know," I said.

"I think it's someone like those construction workers," Erin said.

"So?"

"So aren't you curious about why he called us Betas?" Erin asked. "And what the sample shopper orientation program is? And what kind of writing was on that clipboard?"

"To tell you the truth, Erin," I said, "I'm just glad we got out of there."

10

"I'm going," Erin said that night. She was sitting on the porch steps holding a butterfly net with a long, thin handle. Above her on the outside of the house was a bright lamp with a million little bugs flying crazily around it.

"You can't, Erin," I said.

"Why not?"

"Because those people are weird," I said. "We don't know where they come from. They might hurt you or kidnap you or something."

A decent-sized moth joined the swarm of bugs around the light. Without getting up, Erin swung the net and caught it. A second later it had joined half a dozen other moths fluttering desperately inside a large mayonnaise jar. Tomorrow each of them would become dinner for a toad, frog, or snake.

"They won't hurt me," Erin said.

"How do you know?"

"Because they'll think I'm one of them, just like that personnel man did today," Erin said.

"What if you make a mistake and they catch you?" I asked.

"They'll think I'm one of those dumb Betas," Erin said. "You heard that man. They expect Betas to make mistakes."

"You don't even know where the swamp entrance is," I said.

"Bet you anything it's those doors we saw today," Erin said.

"But you don't know where they go," I said.

Before Erin could answer, something big glided through the light and then back into the shadows.

"*Actias luna!*" Erin gasped and jumped up.

"What?"

"A luna moth," Erin said, peering into the dark. "Oh, please don't go away! Please come back!"

As if it had heard her, the moth flew back into the light again. It was five times the size of the other moths we'd seen and five times as beautiful, too. It had big green wings that tapered off into

54

long tails. It flapped them slowly as if it didn't have the strength to fly faster.

"Isn't it beautiful, Dwight? Isn't it?"

It sure was. I reached for the butterfly net.

"What are you doing?" Erin asked.

"I'm gonna catch it," I said.

Erin grabbed the handle. "No, don't!"

I pulled the net away. "What's wrong with you? Don't you want it?"

The next thing I knew, Erin grabbed the net and dove. Thump! She hit the ground hard, snapping the handle in half. I stood on the porch step and stared at her, thinking she'd really gone nuts. But she was still watching the luna moth. It made one last lazy pass at the light and then disappeared into the dark.

Erin stood up and wiped the dirt off her knees.

"I thought you liked to catch them," I said.

"Not that moth," Erin said, picking up the broken net. "If you catch it in the net you destroy its wings. Didn't you see how delicate it was? I bet it just hatched."

"How do you know that?" I asked.

"Because it was a perfect specimen," Erin said. "In a few weeks the wings will get torn just from the wind and rain."

"That's too bad," I said.

"But before that it will mate so that next year there will be more *Actias lunas*," Erin said. Then she looked off through the dark in the direction of the mall. "That is, if they don't destroy the swamp."

11

The next morning Erin came into my room carrying a brown paper bag.

"I need your help," she said.

"How?"

Erin put the bag on my bed. "I want you to throw this down to me from your window."

I looked in the bag. Inside was Erin's white dress with the pink roses. "Why don't you just wear it?" I asked.

"Because then I'll have to tell Mom that I'm going to a party again," Erin said. "Considering the fact that I never get invited to parties, going to two in two days sounds suspicious."

"Listen," I said. "I really don't think you need this dress. I mean, if you were going shopping at the mall on the east side of town, would you wear a dress?"

Erin shook her head.

"If you don't want anyone to notice you, then you should dress like a shopper," I said.

"You're right," she said. She took the bag and went back to her room. But a minute later she returned.

"If I'm not home by dinnertime, you'll have to make up an excuse for me," she said.

"Why won't you be home by dinnertime?" I asked.

"Well, I don't know how long the sample shopper orientation will take," she said.

"Okay," I said. "I'll try to make something up."

Erin left, but soon she was back again.

"What do you want now?" I asked.

"I was just wondering what you were doing today," she said.

I looked at her and sighed. I knew she'd do anything to try to stop them from paving over the swamp. But she was scared to go back there alone.

"Okay," I said. "I'll go, too."

Erin smiled. "For an older brother, you're not so bad."

When we got to the clearing in the swamp, a small crowd of people were waiting. There were old people, teenagers, mothers with little kids in strollers. They all looked like the kind of people you'd see at a shopping mall. Erin and I stood at the edge of the group.

"You notice anything strange?" Erin whispered.

I shook my head.

"No one has any mud on their shoes," she whispered.

I looked around. She was right.

"Then, how did they get here?" I asked.

Erin nodded at the Dumpster. "And no one's talking either," she said. The whole crowd was just standing there silently. Even the little kids were quiet. They weren't looking around or anything. It was like a wax museum.

"Weird," I whispered.

Standing next to us was an older kid, wearing a Harvard T-shirt and blue jeans.

"Uh, excuse me," Erin said. "Is this the sample shoppers' group?"

The kid nodded.

"How did you get in this group?" Erin asked.

He didn't answer.

"Do you come from around here?" I asked.

The kid acted like he hadn't heard me.

I looked at Erin. "It's weird."

"I think I know what's going on," Erin said. She turned to the kid again. "Are you here for orientation?"

The kid nodded.

"Don't you love a pink sky?" Erin asked.

The kid didn't respond.

"Isn't concrete delicious?" Erin asked.

Again the kid didn't answer.

"Does orientation start at ten A.M.?" Erin asked.

This time the kid nodded.

Erin turned to me. "They only hear what they're supposed to hear," she said. "If you say something that doesn't have to do with being a sample shopper, they don't understand, so they don't answer."

"Do you think they're robots?" I asked.

Before Erin could answer, the metal doors in the sand began to open. A wave of cold air from inside gave me goose bumps. A moment later the personnel man we'd met the day before climbed out and stood in front of the crowd. "Sample shoppers," he said in a loud voice. "You will follow me."

He turned and started to walk. The crowd of sample shoppers followed. Including Erin and me.

12

He led us down the stairs and into a long, narrow tunnel lit with overhead lights. It felt cold inside. Not like a refrigerator, but like air conditioning turned up high. I shivered a little, but no one around me seemed to mind.

"Twenty-eight, twenty-nine, thirty," Erin whispered.

"What are you doing?" I asked.

"Counting how many steps we're taking," she said.

At the end of the tunnel, the personnel man pushed open another door.

"An underground base!" Erin whispered.

She was right. On the other side of the door was a huge complex of desks and glass-walled rooms teeming with activity.

"It looks like NASA headquarters," I whispered.

"And by my estimates, it's right under the mall," Erin whispered back.

The personnel man led us down a corridor lined with busy offices and computer stations crowded with people sitting at display screens. We could hear phones ringing, and the high-pitched whine of printers spewing out information. At the end of the corridor we stopped. The personnel man turned to the crowd. "Please wait for your manager," he said, and then walked away.

Just as they had in the swamp, the crowd stood perfectly still and said nothing. Erin and I looked around. We were surrounded by classrooms lined with glass. In the one closest to us, a woman wearing a gray business suit and glasses was addressing a large group of well-dressed people.

"Our research has shown that salespeople in this system greet shoppers by saying 'Cash or charge?' " the woman said in a loud voice. "Now repeat after me."

All at once the entire room said, "Cash or charge?"

"Very good," said the woman. "Now, at the end of your transaction it is customary to say 'Have a nice day.' Repeat after me."

"Have a nice day," the group repeated.

Erin looked at me and rolled her eyes.

Across the hall in another classroom, the fat security guard we'd seen the day before at the Dumpster was lecturing a group of men and women wearing matching blue uniforms.

"When you suspect someone of shoplifting," the guard said, "you will say, 'Please open your bag.' "

"Please open your bag," the group chanted.

"If they resist," the man said, "or if you discover they have taken something, you will say, 'Please accompany me to the office.' "

"Please accompany me to the office," the group chanted.

"Weird," Erin whispered.

Just then a woman appeared in front of our group. She was lugging two big shopping bags in one hand and in the other hand she had a soda cup with a straw sticking out of it. A pair of sunglasses rested on top of her hair.

"I am your manager," she said. "All sample shoppers follow me." She led us to an empty classroom.

Erin and I followed the group and sat down in plastic chairs. The manager put down the shopping bags and soda cup and stood in front of us. To her left was a large television on a stand.

"Welcome to sample shopping orientation," the woman said. "Our research shows that in this system shoppers do not like to enter stores or restaurants unless there are other shoppers already inside. Therefore it will be your function to eat or shop in any store that would otherwise be empty. You will always work in pairs. When you do see a real shopper enter the store, you will turn to your companion and say, 'I can't believe this store isn't crowded. The prices are great.' "

All around us the sample shoppers chanted, "I can't believe this store isn't crowded. The prices are great."

"Very good," the manager said. "Some of you will also be assigned to walk up and down the halls carrying shopping bags filled with packages. You will say things like, 'My feet are killing me, but I just have to try that store over there.' "

"My feet are killing me," the crowd said, "but I just have to try that store over there."

"Excellent," the woman said.

The lecture lasted for almost an hour. The manager went over everything the sample shoppers had to know. Even how to act lost in the parking lot. Then she looked at her wristwatch.

"In a moment I will instruct you on the uses of currency in this system," she said. "But right now, please pay attention to the monitor. Mr. Abernathy will be addressing us shortly."

The manager turned and faced the television. I noticed that in the other classrooms and offices everyone had stopped what they were doing and were also waiting. Erin gave me a funny look. I shrugged. This place was getting stranger by the second.

After a few moments the room suddenly became dark, and an old man appeared on the television screen. He was wearing blue jeans, a polo shirt, and an old baseball cap. His skin was wrinkled, and his hair was white. He had a gravelly voice, and he sounded very far away.

"Hello, everyone at our new Earth systems headquarters," he said cheerfully.

"Hello, Mr. Abernathy," the sample shoppers replied in a monotone.

"How's it going out there?" the old man asked.

"Great, Mr. Abernathy," everyone droned mechanically.

"That's wonderful, just wonderful," the old man said. "Are you all learning your jobs well?"

"Yes, Mr. Abernathy."

"Excellent. I'll be coming down on Monday morning. I look forward to seeing you all then. Now, is there something you want to say to me?"

The manager stood up and raised her arms. "All

for the mall and the mall for all," the sample shoppers chanted without emotion.

"That's music to my ears," the old man said. "I'll see you on Monday."

The image on the monitor went from the old man to a picture of a dollar bill. "Welcome to the Earth systems currency demonstration," an electronic voice said. "This is a dollar. The basic monetary unit for this system."

A picture of a penny appeared next. "There are one hundred pennies in each dollar," the electronic voice said.

Erin nudged me with her elbow. "Let's get out of here," she whispered, sliding out of her chair. I followed her along the wall to the door. Before I went out, I turned and looked back in the room. Every single pair of eyes was staring at the monitor.

13

Erin and I stepped into the corridor and started walking back toward the tunnel. I was still worried we'd get caught, but the other people in the corridor passed us without a glance.

Erin stopped next to some large framed photographs on the wall. "Dwight, look at these," she said.

I walked over and looked. Each picture was an aerial shot of a huge complex of low buildings and broad parking lots. It took me a second to realize they were malls. Except, instead of covering acres, they covered miles and miles. As far as the eye could see. Each had a name: Demar Mall, Crab Galaxy; Cassiopeia Mall, Triffid Galaxy; Pleiades Mall, Great Zoon Galaxy.

"Do you know what these are?" Erin asked.

"Really big malls," I said.

"They're planets, Dwight," Erin said. "Whole

planets covered by malls. And those are the galaxies they're in."

I stared at her for a second. "Galaxies in space?"

Erin nodded. We must have been thinking the
same thing because we both started to walk
quickly toward the tunnel.

"Hey, you!" someone yelled.

Erin and I jumped around. A real punky-looking
kid with spiked hair and dark glasses was standing in the doorway of a classroom, glaring at us.
He was wearing a black leather jacket and boots
with chains on them.

"You must be the demonstration Betas from
research," he said. "Get in here."

Erin and I looked in the classroom. There were
about one hundred kids and teenagers squeezed
inside.

"Come on," the kid shouted. "What are you
waiting for?"

Not knowing what else to do, Erin and I went
in. Meanwhile, the punky-looking kid went to the
front of the room.

"Okay, you dumb Betas, where was I?" he said.
"Oh, yeah. The research department indicates
that in this mall system a lot of kids hang out at
malls. It's called loitering. That's why you dummies are called sample loiterers, in case you didn't

know. Now I've already gone over some of this with you. What do we say when a security guard tells us to move?"

In unison the crowd chanted, "Buzz off, jerk. It's a free country."

"And what do we say when we're hungry?"

"Let's cop a slice and chow down," the group replied."

"And when we're bored?"

"Wow, this is a drag, man," the crowd said.

The punky kid nodded. "Okay, dummies, now over here we have some junk that kids in this system play with."

He walked over to a big cardboard box in the front of the room and looked into it. He pulled out a Frisbee and scowled.

"I guess this is something they wear on their heads," he said, putting it on his head.

Next he pulled out a skateboard. "From the wheels on the bottom I would assume that this is some kind of transportation."

Next he pulled out a Hacky Sack. "I don't know what this is," he said and tossed it back into the box. Then he turned to Erin and me. "Okay, demonstration team, here's your stuff."

Erin and I looked into the box. There were more Frisbees, skateboards, and Hacky Sacks in it. And a freestyle bike, too. "You're in charge," Erin whispered. "I'll be your assistant."

"Go to the other side of the room," I whispered back. I picked up one of the Frisbees and threw it across the room to Erin, and she threw it back. Next, I demonstrated how to use a Hacky Sack and a skateboard. Finally I got to the freestyle bike and did every flatland trick I could think of. The punky-looking kid seemed interested.

"Wow, this stuff really is cool," he said, picking up one of the Frisbees and trying to throw it. "I wish some of you were normal instead of being dumb Betas. It would be fun to have someone to do some of this stuff with."

Erin and I glanced at each other, but Erin shook her head. Then I had an idea.

"The research department indicates that we don't say cool," I said. "We say rad."

"Rad," the kid repeated.

"And to be authentic," I said, "the Betas must practice."

"All right, you dumb Betas," the kid said. "It's time to practice."

The next thing I knew, everyone in the classroom was practicing something. Frisbees were flying everywhere. Hacky Sacks were bouncing off people's heads. Skateboarders were crashing into chairs. Freestylists were crashing into skateboarders. Even the punky kid was getting into it.

Then Erin nudged me. "Look who just came in," she said.

I looked at the door and saw a guy and a girl. They were both wearing jeans. The guy had on a white T-shirt, and his jeans had holes in the knees. The girl was wearing a Hawaiian shirt and sunglasses. They looked serious.

The punky kid rode up to them on a freestyling bike. "Hey, what's happening?"

"We are the loitering demonstration team," the guy said.

"Impossible, man, they're already here," the punky kid said.

"We have our requisition orders," the girl said, pulling a piece of paper out of her jeans.

The punky kid turned toward us. "Do you have papers?"

"Well, uh, we left ours at home," I said.

"Home?" the kid frowned. "What home?"

I glanced at Erin, hoping she could bail us out of this one.

"Uh, actually we're the preliminary loitering demonstration team," Erin said. She pointed at the guy and girl. "They must be the advanced team. As you can see, the Betas have now progressed to the advanced stage."

Behind us, the Betas had begun to mix things up. One of them was standing on a Frisbee. Another was trying to throw a skateboard to someone across the room.

"I'm sure they'll be very glad to see you," Erin said. She tugged my sleeve, and we started to inch toward the exit.

"I wasn't told about a preliminary team," the punky kid said.

"Of course you were," Erin said, inching toward the door. "Check your papers."

The kid looked down at the sheet of paper in his hands, and Erin and I ran.

"Hey, wait!" he shouted after us.

We got out to the corridor.

"Stop!" the punky kid shouted. "Don't go!"

We pushed through the doors that led to the tunnel and ran. A few seconds later we pushed open the metal doors leading to the swamp. We were free.

14

Erin and I rode toward home without talking. It seemed like there was a lot to talk about, but it was all so crazy that I felt nervous about bringing it up.

Erin was the one who finally said it: "They're not from here."

"I know," I said.

"No one from here would have to learn how to shop and use money," Erin said. "Everyone already knows that stuff."

"I know," I said.

"But if they're not from here," Erin said, "then where are they from?"

"That I don't know," I said.

Erin and I got home. I probably should have gone over to Sean's to see the freestyle ramp, but I didn't feel like it. How can you go fool around at your friend's house when there may be people from another planet at your local mall?

We went into the kitchen. I poured myself a glass of Coke, and Erin had orange juice. We sat at the kitchen table, drinking and thinking. It sort of reminded me of Mom and Dad.

"Maybe we're imagining too much," I said. "Maybe they are from here, but they're just weird."

"What about those malls on other planets in other galaxies?" Erin asked.

"Maybe it's some kind of joke," I said. "Or they're making a movie or something."

"Be serious, Dwight," Erin said.

I had to sigh. "You really saw that Dumpster land here?" I asked.

"I swear, Dwight."

We were quiet again for a while. I wiped the condensation off the side of my glass with my finger. Erin chewed on her thumb a little. I had a feeling we were both thinking the same thing.

"If we tell anyone about this," I said, "they'll think we're crazy."

Erin nodded.

"But if we don't tell anyone, those people in the mall will just do whatever they're here to do," I said.

74

"They're going to turn this whole planet into a mall," Erin said.

"Why?" I asked.

Erin shook her head. In a way it was reassuring to see that she didn't know everything.

"If you had a choice between Mom and Dad, which would you want to tell?" she asked.

I shrugged. "They'll both think we're crazy."

"I agree," Erin said. "But if you had to choose which one you wanted to think we were crazy, which would you choose?"

That I had to think about.

Erin started to get up.

"Where are you going?" I asked.

"The store," she said.

"You're going to tell them?" I asked.

"I have to, Dwight."

"Which one?"

"I don't know," Erin said. "I guess I'll see who's in a better mood."

15

Not many people go downtown to shop anymore. Two of the stores on the block where Osborn's Records is are empty and have FOR RENT signs in the window. My father used to keep the store open until nine some nights, but one night a man came in with a gun and made him empty the cash register. Now he always closes at six.

My mother works at the store four afternoons a week. She was at the cash register in front when Erin and I got there. She looked bored.

"What are you two doing here?" she asked.

"Uh, we just came to visit," Erin said.

Mom scowled. We didn't come to the store very often. "Do you want something?"

"Uh, no," Erin said. "Where's Dad?"

"He's in the office in the back," Mom said.

"Okay." Erin started walking down the aisles of record racks. There was only one shopper, a bald-headed man, in the store.

"What are you doing?" I whispered.

"I guess I'm going to tell Dad," Erin whispered back.

"Why?"

"Well, you saw Mom just now," Erin said. "Would you have told her?"

"No."

Dad's office was in the storage room behind a curtain at the back of the store. The room was filled with cardboard boxes of records. Dad was sitting at a table covered with papers. He was studying rows of numbers on a computer screen.

"Well, look who's here," he said.

"Hi, Dad, how's business?" Erin asked.

"It stinks," Dad said. "How come you want to know?"

Erin glanced at me and then sat down on a couple of boxes. "I don't really," she said. "But there is something we want to talk to you about."

"What is it?"

"Well, it's going to sound kind of strange," Erin began.

"Totally crazy is more like it," I said.

"But we wouldn't tell you if we didn't really believe it," Erin said.

"We've seen it with our own eyes," I said.

"So we just want you to listen with an open mind," Erin said.

Dad nodded. Erin turned and looked at me like she didn't know where to begin. I couldn't help her.

"Come on," Dad said. "I'm dying from the suspense."

"We think there's something really strange going on over at that new mall," Erin said. She told him about the Galactic companies, the Dumpster, the doors in the sand, and the construction workers. She didn't mention going underground or what we saw there. Still, by the end of the story I knew Dad must have thought she was a raving lunatic. He looked at me.

"It's true, Dad," I said. "I saw everything except the Dumpster fly. But I looked inside it, and I believe Erin."

Dad took a deep breath and let it out slowly. "Okay," he said. "I'd better take a look."

After telling Mom he was taking us out for an ice cream, Dad put our bikes in the back of his car and we drove over to the mall. We parked in the dirt lot at Patton Field and then walked toward the swamp. Erin wanted to show him the Dumpster first.

"Just promise me this isn't a joke," Dad said as he took his first step in the mud.

"I promise," Erin said. She led him through the swamp and I followed. Gnats buzzed around Dad's head and he kept swatting mosquitoes away. His shoes were caked with mud. It seemed as if Erin was taking longer than usual to find the sandy clearing. After a while my father glanced back at me impatiently. All I could do was shrug.

Finally Erin stopped in the middle of a bog. "They hid it."

"What?" Dad said incredulously.

Erin started slogging around in ankle-deep mud. "They hid it. The Dumpster, the sandy clearing. . . . They got rid of them."

Dad gave her a look. Erin picked up a stick and started poking around through the mud for the metal doors.

"Darn it," she said. "They've hidden everything."

Dad was looking pretty annoyed.

"Honest, Dad," I said. "It was all here; I swear I saw it."

Dad waited a few minutes more while Erin and

I poked around with sticks, but we couldn't find anything.

"We can still go to the mall and show Dad the construction workers," Erin said.

We walked through the swamp toward the mall. As we came out of the trees, Erin gasped. A line of dump trucks were unloading landfill at the edge of the swamp, and two big bulldozers were pushing and spreading it. Nearby a thick black hose snaked its way out of the swamp to a large yellow pump spewing water into a storm drain.

"They're draining it!" Erin shouted. For a second I thought she was going to attack the pump with her fists, but she stopped and took a deep breath.

"Are you sure we should be here?" Dad asked, looking at the trucks and bulldozers.

"Don't worry, they can't see us," Erin said.

"Can't see us?" Dad repeated, scowling.

"Can I help you?" a deep voice asked.

We turned around. Standing behind us was the heavyset security guard we'd seen at the Dumpster, the one who'd given the lecture to the other security guards that morning.

"Hello, John," Dad said, shaking the security guard's hand.

"Oh, hello, Mr. Osborn," the security guard said.

Erin looked stunned. "You know each other?"

"Sure," Dad said. "John used to be the security guard over at Longerin's Jewelers in town before they closed down."

"I was sorry to see them go," John said.

"So you're working over here?" Dad asked.

"Yup," said John. "I'm head of security. Now, what can I do for you folks?"

"I want my father to see what's under this mall," Erin said.

John looked surprised. "Why, there's nothing except rock and dirt under it."

"That's not true," Erin said. "There's a whole lower level down there where they give classes on how to act like humans."

John glanced at my father. "I'm sorry, but I don't know what she's talking about."

"You do, too," Erin said. "We went down there this morning. The door from the swamp leads down there."

John glanced at my father. I knew the look.

"We're sorry to have bothered you, John," my father said. "I think we'll go now. Congratulations on your new job."

"Thanks, Mr. Osborn."

Dad didn't say anything on the way home. He dropped us off at our house and then drove back to the store. Erin ran upstairs and slammed the door to her room. I sat in the living room and watched TV. It was only a matter of time, I figured, until the men in white came with straitjackets and took us away.

16

That night at dinner Dad pretended nothing had happened. I figured that was a good idea and pretended, too, but Erin just sat close-mouthed through the whole meal and sulked.

About an hour later I went into the kitchen to get a frozen fruit bar. Erin was standing on the stepladder, pulling a five-pound bag of sugar out of the pantry.

"What are you doing?" I asked.

She put her finger to her lips and then turned and went out the screen door in the back. I figured she'd wait for me there, but when I went out back I saw that she was cutting around to the front of the house.

"Hey, Erin," I said, and jogged after her. I caught up to her on the sidewalk.

"Don't try to stop me," she said.

"Stop you from what?" I asked. "Where are you going with all that sugar?"

"I'm going to make sure that pump doesn't take one more ounce of water from the swamp."

"Hey, that's vandalism," I said.

"That's what you call it," Erin said. "I call it saving the lives of thousands of harmless creatures who never hurt anyone."

"Listen, Erin, you can't take on that whole mall yourself. You saw what they did today. They can switch everything around. No one's going to believe us. I'm not even sure I believe it anymore. We're just lucky Dad's willing to let it go."

"Well, I'm not," Erin said, marching down the street toward the mall. It was just starting to get dark.

"Jamming the pump won't stop them," I said.

"I'll find a way," Erin said.

"Like what?"

"Remember that announcement from Mr. Abernathy this morning?" Erin said. "I don't know who he is, but he sounds important. He's coming here Monday, and I'm going to be there when he arrives."

"You could get in a lot of trouble," I said. "What if I tell Mom and Dad?"

"Then, I'll pretend I don't know what you're talking about, and they'll think you're crazy." She started to run. I watched her disappear into the dark. I knew I couldn't stop her.

17

Early Saturday morning I got out of bed and went downstairs like I was thirsty and wanted to get a drink of water. I even opened the kitchen cabinet and clinked some glasses in case Mom or Dad was awake. But I doubted they would be. They usually slept late on Saturdays. Then I very quietly opened the kitchen door and went out.

The night before, I'd left some clothes in a bag under the porch. I got them out and got dressed. Then I got my bike and quietly walked it across the lawn to the street.

Sean was waiting for me down the street. He was wearing green rubber boots. His eyes were puffy, and he was yawning.

"You ready?" I asked.

Sean nodded. "Can you tell me what this is all about?"

"Not yet, but soon," I said. "Let's go." As we

rode toward the swamp, I noticed that he no longer had the cast.

"How's your arm?" I asked.

Sean rubbed his wrist. "It feels okay, but the doc says I have to do exercises to strengthen it."

We rode past Patton Field. The grass on the baseball diamond was dried out and brown, and tall weeds were growing in the outfield.

"Do you ever play here?" Sean asked.

"In the fall sometimes," I said. "It's hard to get enough kids for teams in the summer because everyone goes to camp. Besides, in the summer it gets really dry and dusty."

"How come you don't go to camp?" Sean asked.

"We used to," I said. "But then that mall on the east side of town opened, and the record store there started taking away some of my dad's business, and he couldn't afford to send us anymore."

"In California there are a lot of town recreation facilities," Sean said. "So even if you don't go to camp, there's still plenty to do."

"I wish they had that here," I said. "But all we've got is Patton Field."

We got to the swamp and plodded through the mud. By now I had been there enough times to know where the mud wasn't too deep. Sean looked around in wonder.

"Wow, this is a weird place," he said.

"You want to see something cool?" I said. "Look at this."

I pointed at a big tree. Sean stared at it. At first he didn't see anything, but then he recognized the outline of a large moth with its wings spread against the bark. It looked so much like the tree that most people wouldn't have noticed it.

"That's rad," Sean said, staring at it.

"We better keep going," I said.

A little while later we came to the clearing. Just as I'd expected, everything was back — the sand, the door, and the Dumpster. I didn't know how they hid all that stuff the day before, and I didn't care.

"What's this doing here?" Sean asked, pointing at the Dumpster.

I put my fingers to my lips. That security guard, John, might have been around. "It's a long story," I whispered. "I'll explain it later. But right now I want you to look at the inside."

"How come?" Sean asked.

"You'll see."

Sean climbed up and looked inside the Dumpster while I stayed outside and watched for any "visitors."

"Oh, wow, radical!" Sean gasped as he looked

over the side and into the Dumpster. "Where'd this come from?"

"I'll explain that later, too," I said. "Right now I have one question."

"What?" Sean asked.

"Do you think you can fly this thing?"

18

On Monday morning Erin and I went down to the living room. Mom was doing her aerobics.

"Twenty-four," the record said.

"Unh," said Mom.

"Twenty-five."

"Unh."

"We're gonna spend the day in the swamp, Mom," Erin said.

"Twenty-six."

"Unh. Do you want me to make you some sandwiches?" Mom asked.

"We already made them," I said.

"We'll see you around dinner," Erin said.

"Twenty-seven."

"Unh. Okay, kids, have a good time."

We got on our bikes and rode to the swamp. Sean and Dickie were waiting there for us. They were both wearing rubber boots.

"You guys ready?" I asked.

Sean nodded. Dickie was chewing nervously on his fingernails. He looked scared.

"What if your plan doesn't work?" he asked.

"We told our mother where we were going," I said. "If we're not home by dinner, she'll call the police."

"But if these guys are really aliens," Dickie said, "we could be on some planet a zillion miles away from here by then."

"You're right, we could," Erin said. "So are you coming or not?"

Dickie swallowed. "I guess."

We went into the swamp and found the sandy clearing. The Dumpster wasn't there. Erin showed Dickie the blind she'd built in one of the trees, and he climbed up into it. The rest of us hid in the brush near the clearing.

"What time is it?" I whispered.

"Ten of ten," Erin whispered back.

"Should be any time now," I said.

Sure enough, a few minutes later we heard a soft whirring sound. Then the Dumpster appeared just above the treetops and began to descend slowly toward the clearing.

"I don't believe this," Dickie whimpered in the tree.

The Dumpster landed, and the top opened. The old man, Mr. Abernathy, got out. No sooner had his feet touched the ground than the metal doors in the sand slowly began to open. Mr. Abernathy stepped in and went down the stairs. The doors began to close.

"All clear," Dickie hissed from above.

Sean, Erin, and I jumped up and ran to the doors. I stuck a stick between them before they could close.

Erin knelt down and put her ear to the crack between the doors. "I hear his footsteps," she whispered.

We waited.

"Okay," Erin whispered. "I don't hear them anymore. He must be inside the base."

"Let's open it," I said.

The metal door was heavy, but Sean, Erin, and I managed to pull it open.

"Think you can hold it by yourself?" I asked Sean.

"Yeah," he said.

Erin and I looked at each other. I swallowed. "You ready?"

She nodded.

"Okay, let's do it."

19

Erin and I climbed down the stairs. We both watched as Sean closed the door on the stick again, allowing a thin crack of daylight in. Then we turned and walked down the long tunnel to the base.

The base itself was almost deserted. The offices and workstations were being manned by a skeleton crew. The printers weren't printing, and the phones were quiet. Erin and I stood in the wide corridor, looking around.

"Where could they be?" I asked.

"Wait," Erin said. "Listen." Coming from the far end of the corridor was a faint voice. It sounded like someone addressing a group. Erin and I quickly went down the corridor until we reached a pair of double doors at the end.

"*Our new Earth systems mall will be the big-*

gest and best ever," the voice was saying. *"At completion it will cover more than twenty-six million square miles and will provide jobs for nearly two billion employees."*

I pulled open the door a crack and peeked in. Inside was a large, darkened auditorium full of people. On the stage in front, the managers were sitting in a row of chairs. Next to them Mr. Abernathy stood at a podium, illuminated by a single spotlight.

"The air conditioning alone will use up more than a billion kilowatts of electricity a day," Mr. Abernathy said. *"More than a million slices of pizza will be sold every hour."*

I pulled open the door some more, and Erin and I slipped into the auditorium. In the dim light I could see that we were near the section where the sample shoppers were sitting. We took seats with them.

"Half a billion gallons of water will be consumed each day at water fountains," Mr. Abernathy said.

Erin took a deep breath and cupped her hands around her mouth. "By whom?" she shouted.

The auditorium became silent. Mr. Abernathy looked stunned. On the stage some of the managers jumped up.

"If the whole planet is a mall, who will be left to shop at it?" Erin shouted.

The managers were talking hastily among themselves. The spotlight left the old man and began to sweep across the audience. It swept over us, but Erin and I remained stock-still like the Betas around us.

"Who said that?" Mr. Abernathy said. *"Identify yourself."*

"I'm Erin Osborn," Erin shouted. "A native of this planet. And I'm asking you to stop before you destroy it."

"Destroy it?" Mr. Abernathy said. *"Nonsense. We wish to improve it. When this mall is completed, nearly forty percent of the planet's surface will be air-conditioned. Poverty will be eliminated. From the age of twelve up, everyone who wants to will have a job at the mall. Except for some shoplifting and petty vandalism, crime will be virtually eliminated."*

"And eventually everyone will become living, breathing robots like these Betas," Erin shouted back.

By now John, the manager of security, had jumped off the stage and was shouting instructions to the Beta security guards. They got up from their seats and began to encircle the audience.

"And what about all the animals on this planet?" Erin shouted. "All the reptiles and amphibians and mammals and birds and insects. Where are they going to go when the world is one big mall?"

Mr. Abernathy did not answer. Instead, the lights went on all over the auditorium. Erin glanced at her watch. It was time. She and I stood up.

"Arrest those two," Mr. Abernathy said.

20

I guess they didn't have anything that resembled a jail because they took us to an empty office under the mall. Inside were four blank white walls and a few plastic chairs. Erin and I sat down, and two security guards were stationed outside the office. In our plan, we hoped Mr. Abernathy would come and talk to us, but it looked like he was going to continue his speech.

Erin sat in her chair, looking glum. "Now that I think of it," she said, "I guess it was dumb to think he'd bother with us unless he had to."

"Yeah," I said.

"I guess we'll just have to wait."

But a few moments later the door to the office opened. In came the punky guy from the loitering class. He looked excited.

"I knew you guys were really Earthlings," he said.

"What are you?"

"Me?" the guy said. "I'm an Abernathy."

"What's that?" I asked.

"Where I come from there are Abernathys and Betas," he said. "Abernathys run everything, and Betas are the employees. All the Abernathys are related to Mr. Abernathy. I'm his grandson. You can call me Tom."

"Where do you come from?" Erin asked.

"Mall," Tom said. "It's a planet in the Quintary Galaxy, about eighty-six billion light years from here."

"Why do you look like a human?" Erin asked.

"We always take on the characteristics of the mall-building life form on the planet we're assigned to," Tom said. "But you're the closest life form to our natural state I've ever seen. You should have seen me on Finiturist in the Turgid Galaxy. I had green scales and a tail. It was a drag. To tell you the truth, being an Abernathy is a drag."

"How come?" I asked.

"Because all we do is follow Grandpa from planet to planet turning them into malls," Tom said. "I don't have any friends. I don't have anyone to do anything with. That's why I didn't want you guys to leave the other day. You're the first intelligent beings I've ever met outside the family. Grandpa says I'm going to take over the business when he retires, but forget it. There's no way."

"Why is it so important to him to turn planets into malls?" I asked.

"You heard him," Tom said. "He thinks it's the only way to eliminate crime and wipe out poverty."

"But when people spend all their time in malls, they turn into Betas," Erin said. "They can't think for themselves, and they can't talk about anything except the mall. All their needs are met, so they sink into a state of obliviousness."

"You're telling me," Tom said. "The only way you can get a Beta excited is to announce a sale."

The office door opened, and Mr. Abernathy came in. He saw Tom and frowned.

"Tom," he said. "What are you doing here?"

"I had to talk to these two humans," Tom said. "I couldn't believe there were people my own age with brains."

Mr. Abernathy sighed and looked at Erin and me. "I don't know what to do with you two. I can't let you go because you'll probably tell other Earthlings, and our whole operation might be discovered."

"I sure hope so," Erin said.

"On the other hand," Mr. Abernathy said, "it's against my nature to keep anyone against their will. One of the beauties of mall development is that people come because they want to."

"Because, when the whole world is a mall, there's no place else to go," Erin said.

"Young lady," Mr. Abernathy said, "why are you so adamantly anti-mall?"

"Because your mall is going to put my father out of business and is going to destroy the homes of millions of animals."

"Your father will find work at the mall," Mr. Abernathy said. "And as for those animals, some will come to live in pet shops. The others will not be missed."

Erin's jaw dropped. But before she could reply, the door opened again and Dickie came in, followed by John, the head of security.

"Found this one out in the corridor," John said.

Dickie's face was red and he looked scared. But he also winked at Erin.

"Oh, wonderful," Mr. Abernathy said. "I wonder how many more Earthlings know about us."

"One more," Erin said. "And he's got your Dumpster."

21

Mr. Abernathy sent John to see if it was true. He was back a few minutes later. "The Dumpster is gone."

The color drained out of Mr. Abernathy's face. "What kind of childish prank is this?" he asked angrily.

"It's not a prank," Erin said. "You can have the Dumpster back."

"I can?" Mr. Abernathy asked.

"Yes," said Erin. "But first you have to come with us."

"Where?" Mr. Abernathy asked.

"To see why we don't want you to turn this planet into a mall," Erin said.

"It's a trick," John, the security man, said. "I have spent a year on this planet studying its culture. Dishonesty and deceit are second nature to it."

"That's not true," Erin said. "Some people are deceitful. But not everyone. We're not all the same like your Betas. Each human being is an individual. And I for one am neither dishonest nor deceitful."

"All right, let's get on with this," Mr. Abernathy said impatiently. "I'm supposed to be at the Fallon Mall in the Catalina Galaxy tomorrow morning, and if I don't get that Dumpster back soon, I'm going to be late."

"Then, I suggest we make a trade," John said. "Mr. Abernathy will go with you, but we will keep this Earthling here until he returns." He pointed at Dickie.

"Why me?" Dickie asked.

I patted him on the shoulder. "Don't worry. One way or the other we won't be long."

"I'm coming, too," Tom said.

"I would rather you stayed here," Mr. Abernathy said. "There's nothing out there to see except a bunch of disorganized people, living in a disorganized world."

"Aw, I never get to go anywhere," Tom whined.

"I think you're afraid of what he'll see," Erin said. "You're afraid he'll like it."

Mr. Abernathy took off his old baseball cap and

rubbed his head. He squinted at Erin. "You think you're pretty smart, young lady."

"Yes, I do," Erin said.

Mr. Abernathy turned to his grandson. "Okay, Tom, you can come."

Tom grinned. "Great!"

We left Dickie and the others in the office and walked down the long tunnel to the metal doors in the sand.

"In all my years of building malls," Mr. Abernathy said, "I've never met resistance quite as clever as this."

"I think it's about time someone stood up to you," Tom said.

Mr. Abernathy pressed his lips together and frowned. But he didn't yell at Tom.

"How long have you been building malls?" Erin asked.

"Ever since I was a boy," Mr. Abernathy said. "My grandfather started, and I learned from him. I hope someday young Tom here will take over."

"No way," Tom said.

"Why do you keep doing it?" I asked.

"A man's got to keep busy, son," Mr. Abernathy said. "Idle hands are the devil's tool."

"Hasn't anyone tried to stop you?"

"Oh, there's always some resistance from misguided folks like yourselves who don't understand," Mr. Abernathy said. "But the malls just keep growing until there's no one left to fight."

"I'll fight this as long as I live," Erin said.

We arrived at the metal doors. The old man touched a spot next to the wall, and the doors opened. We climbed out.

"My, it's hot today," Mr. Abernathy said, pulling back the baseball cap and wiping his brow. It didn't feel that hot to me.

"You're used to air conditioning," Erin told the old man.

"Did you ever see a mall without it?" Mr. Abernathy asked back.

Erin led us across the sand and into the swamp. She began telling Tom and Mr. Abernathy about all the animals that lived there. I listened with one ear, but at the same time I couldn't help wondering where Sean had gone with the Dumpster.

"This swamp is like a whole world to these animals," Erin said. "If you pave it over, you will destroy the homes of thousands of creatures."

"Hmmm." Mr. Abernathy didn't seem very moved by Erin's story. He was more involved in trying to scrape the mud off his cowboy boots with a stick. Tom was busy swatting away mosquitoes.

"If this is what the whole planet's like, forget it," Tom said. "I'd rather be back underground."

"I think we better head toward town," I said.

We walked out of the swamp. It was cloudy and cool out. Erin looked worried. It had never occurred to us that we might not be able to convince Mr. Abernathy to change his mind.

We passed Patton Field. There was a little league game in progress. One team was wearing red and white uniforms. The other team wore green and yellow. They all had baseball caps on. Mr. Abernathy suddenly stopped.

"What is it?" Erin asked.

"This reminds me of something," Mr. Abernathy said.

"What are they doing?" Tom asked.

"Playing a game called baseball," I said.

"If it's a game, why do they need so many players?" Tom asked. "And where are the video screens?"

"There are no screens," I said. "All you need is a bat and a ball."

"And everyone plays together?" Tom asked.

"Sure," I said.

"I really think we ought to get to town," Erin said.

"No, wait," said Mr. Abernathy. "I think I used

to play a game like this when I was a very young boy." He walked over to the small set of rickety wood bleachers next to the field and sat down. Erin, Tom, and I followed and sat down next to him. Mr. Abernathy seemed transfixed.

As we watched, a kid on the field hit a home run. As he sped around the bases, his baseball cap fell off. His teammates cheered.

"Wow, that looks like fun," Tom said.

"As I recall, it was," Mr. Abernathy said.

The kid who'd gotten the hit ran back on the field to get his cap. As he picked it up, Mr. Abernathy took the old baseball cap off his head and stared at it.

"It's the same kind of cap," Tom said.

The old man nodded. "I've never quite understood why I kept this cap all these years. I guess it reminded me of those happy days when I was a boy."

"Whatever happened to the game on our planet?" Tom asked.

"I guess it was covered by the mall," Mr. Abernathy said.

"Think of all the kids who'll never get to play if you cover the world with a mall," I said.

"Yeah, like me," said Tom.

Mr. Abernathy didn't reply. We watched the

game for a while. The sun came out from behind a cloud, and the old man pulled the brim of his cap low. Tom shielded his eyes with his hands. Suddenly I had an idea and started to slide off the bench.

"Where are you going?" Erin asked.

"Don't worry," I said, "I'll be right back."

22

Ten minutes later I was back with a bat, a softball, and two mitts.

"Want to play baseball?" I asked Tom.

"Would I ever!" Tom said, jumping down from the bleacher.

"How about you?" Erin asked Mr. Abernathy.

"Oh, no," he said, shaking his head. "I'm too old."

"But you liked playing when you were young, didn't you?" Erin said, pulling him by the hand. "Come on, it'll be fun."

Mr. Abernathy reluctantly agreed and climbed off the bleacher. He and Erin threw the ball back and forth in front of the bleacher while I showed Tom how to hold the bat and swing.

"Okay, let's try it," I said when I thought Tom had the idea. "Mr. Abernathy can pitch. Tom will bat, Erin will catch, and I'll play the outfield."

Mr. Abernathy managed to get the first few pitches over the plate. Tom swung at them, but he missed.

"Aw, this isn't any fun." He threw the bat to the ground.

"Wait," I said, running in from the outfield. "You can't just quit. It takes practice to get good."

"Who wants to practice?" Tom said. "When you play video games in the mall, you get a score right away. I want to be good right now."

Erin looked at me like she was praying I'd know what to say. But I didn't. Tom looked really discouraged. He even kicked the bat on the ground.

"Now, Tom," Mr. Abernathy said. "Anything truly good in life takes practice. Those video games in the mall let you score right away, but you get bored with them, don't you?"

Tom nodded.

"Once you learn to play baseball, you'll never be bored," I said. It was a bit of an exaggeration, but I figured that if he eventually learned basketball and football as well, it would be hard to get bored.

"Look," I said, picking up the bat. "Pitch one in, Mr. Abernathy." Mr. Abernathy threw a ball in, and I hit it as hard as I could. The ball sailed way up into the air.

"Oh, wow," Tom said, reaching for the bat. "Let me try again."

On the next swing he hit a grounder. "Did you see that?" he yelled excitedly.

Even Mr. Abernathy smiled. "Good hit," he said.

For a while Tom hit and I played the outfield. By then, the little league game had ended and the kids had left the field.

"Couldn't we play a real game?" Tom asked, pointing at the baseball diamond.

"We don't have enough players," I said.

"Then, I'll never really get to play," Tom said. "All I'll ever be able to do is practice."

"Why don't we get some people from the mall?" Erin asked. "If we got all the Abernathys, we'd have enough for teams."

"No, we can't," Mr. Abernathy said. "It's not scheduled."

"Who cares?" Tom asked. "This is fun, Grandpa."

"It's play, Tom," Mr. Abernathy said. "It's not a man's work."

"Oh, give me a break," Tom said. "All I've done my whole life is man's work. It's time to have some fun." And before his grandfather could stop him, Tom ran back toward the swamp.

It was the craziest game of baseball you ever saw. None of the Abernathys really understood how to play, but they all had a great time. The managers of the loiterers and sample shoppers became the Loppers, and the guards and salespeople became the Geoples. Dickie, Erin, and I were the umpires, and the Betas sat in the bleachers and cheered on cue.

They played all afternoon. In the end the Loppers beat the Geoples 23 to 17, but everyone was happy.

"That was the most fun I've ever had," John, the security guard, said, rubbing his back.

"We should really play again soon," said Claire, the manager in charge of the salespeople.

Mr. Abernathy rubbed his arm. It had gotten sore from pitching. "We will," he said.

"When?" Tom asked. "This is the only planet that has this game, and you're going to cover it with another dumb mall."

"We'll leave space for a few baseball fields," Mr. Abernathy said.

"But tomorrow we're going to Fallon," Tom said. "That planet doesn't have this game."

"So we'll leave a few fields there as well," Mr. Abernathy said.

"Instead of building malls, why don't you build baseball stadiums?" Erin said. "You could build them all over the universe. Then, wherever you went, you'd always be able to play."

"That sounds like a good idea," said John, the guard.

"You could build big sports complexes with football, basketball, tennis — all the sports," Dickie said.

"And then people wouldn't turn into Betas," Tom said. "I'd have some friends."

"You could start by turning this mall into a sports complex," I said. "That's what we really need here."

Mr. Abernathy was still rubbing his sore arm. "Well, I don't know about that."

"Oh, come on, Grandpa," Tom said. "I'm so bored with malls, I hope I never see another one for as long as I live."

"He's got a point," said John. "A number of us have gotten pretty tired of building the same malls over and over again. We've been meaning to talk to you about building something else."

Mr. Abernathy thought it over. "Well, to tell you the truth, it has gotten rather dull."

"Then you'll build a sports complex instead?" I asked.

"Could I build one huge one that would cover the whole planet?" Mr. Abernathy asked.

"No," Erin said. "You should only build them in places where people want them. And you can't pave over the swamp."

Mr. Abernathy sighed. "Well, all right."

Everyone cheered. Even the Betas.

23

A few nights later I had a dream that I was in a baseball stadium in the middle of a baseball game when a big Dumpster flew by. Tom stuck his head out and waved, and I yelled, "Come play some baseball the next time you're in the solar system."

"Wake up, Dwight," someone said. I opened my eyes to find Erin shaking my arm.

"What . . . ?"

Erin put her finger to her lips. "Shhh. Listen."

Downstairs I could hear Dad yelling. "Honey! Come here and look at this! You won't believe it!"

"It's the Sunday paper," Erin whispered.

Erin and I went downstairs. Mom and Dad were sitting together, staring down at the paper.

"What's all the yelling about?" Erin asked.

"They're not going to build that new mall," Dad

said. "They're going to build a sports complex instead."

"So?" Erin said, playing dumb.

"Well, your mom and I never told you this," Dad said. "But we were worried that another record store might put Osborn's Records out of business. Now we don't have to worry."

Erin and I looked at the paper. The headline read: NEW MALL TO BECOME SPORTS FACILITY. Under it was a big story and a photo of Mr. Abernathy.

"Gee, Dad, that's great," I said.

Mom and Dad must have read the article twice, just to make sure it was true.

"Let's all go out to brunch and celebrate," Dad said. He and Mom were so happy they didn't even bother to read the rest of the paper. Instead they went upstairs to change.

"We should get dressed," I said.

"Wait," Erin said, thumbing through the paper.

"What are you looking for?" I asked.

"This," Erin said, pointing to a story on page three: FLYING DUMPSTER SIGHTINGS STILL A MYSTERY.

"Sean must have had a great time," I said, as Erin tore the story out and ripped it into tiny pieces.

"It was a good thing he came back in time for Mr. Abernathy to fly to Fallon," Erin said.

"Do you think Mr. Abernathy will keep his word?" I asked.

"I hope so," Erin said.

"So do I," I said. "But every time I go to a mall and see a Dumpster in the back, I know I'll stop and wonder."

About the Author

TODD STRASSER is one of today's most popular young adult novelists. With a blend of fantasy, reality, and humor, his stories reflect concern for the problems young people face. Twice winner of the YASD Best Book award, two of his ten books have been made into movies.

Strasser works in New York City, where he lives with his wife and daughter. He is a frequent speaker at schools, conventions, and meetings of teachers and librarians. With all that to keep him busy, he still finds time to run his own fortune-cookie company.

Delicious New Apples®

Exciting Series for You!

ANIMAL INN™ by Virginia Vail

When 13-year-old Val Taylor comes home from school, she spends her afternoons with a menagerie of horses, dogs, and cats–the residents of Animal Inn, her dad's veterinary clinic.

PETS ARE FOR KEEPS #1	**$2.50 / $3.50 Can.**
A KID'S BEST FRIEND #2	**$2.50 / $3.50 Can.**
MONKEY BUSINESS #3	**$2.50 / $3.50 Can.**

THE BABY-SITTERS CLUB™ by Ann M. Martin

Meet Kristy, Claudia, Mary Anne, and Stacey...the four members of the Baby-sitters Club! They're 7th graders who get involved in all kinds of adventures–with school, boys, and, of course, baby-sitting!

FREE
Baby-sitters Kit!
Details in Books 1, 2, and 3

KRISTY'S GREAT IDEA #1	**$2.50 / $3.50 Can.**
CLAUDIA AND THE PHANTOM PHONE CALLS #2	**$2.50 / $3.50 Can.**
THE TRUTH ABOUT STACEY #3	**$2.50 / $3.50 Can.**
MARY ANNE SAVES THE DAY #4	**$2.50 / $3.50 Can.**

APPLE® CLASSICS

Kids everywhere have loved these stories for a long time...and so will you!

THE CALL OF THE WILD by Jack London
After being stolen from his home, Buck–part St. Bernard, part German Shepherd–returns to the wild...as the leader of a wolf pack!   **$2.50 / $3.95 Can.**

LITTLE WOMEN by Louisa May Alcott (abridged)
The March sisters were more than just sisters–they were friends! You'll never forget Meg, Jo, Beth, and Amy.   **$2.50 / $3.95 Can.**

WHITE FANG by Jack London
White Fang–half dog, half wolf–is captured by the Indians, tortured by a cowardly man, and he becomes a fierce, deadly fighter. Will he ever find a loving master?
$2.50 / $3.50 Can.

Look in your bookstores now for these great titles!

■ Scholastic Books   APP871

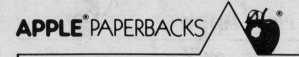
APPLE® PAPERBACKS

Delicious Reading!

NEW APPLE® TITLES $2.50 each

☐ FM 40382-6 **Oh Honestly, Angela!** Nancy K. Robinson

☐ FM 40305-2 **Veronica the Show-Off** Nancy K. Robinson

☐ FM 33662-2 **DeDe Takes Charge!** Johanna Hurwitz

☐ FM 40180-7 **Sixth Grade Can Really Kill You** Barthe DeClements

☐ FM 40874-7 **Stage Fright** Ann M. Martin

☐ FM 40513-6 **Witch Lady Mystery** Carol Beach York

☐ FM 40452-0 **Ghosts Who Went to School** Judith Spearing

☐ FM 33946-X **Swimmer** Harriet May Savitz

☐ FM 40406-7 **Underdog** Marilyn Sachs

BEST-SELLING APPLE® TITLES

☐ FM 40725-2 **Nothing's Fair in Fifth Grade** Barthe DeClements

☐ FM 40466-0 **The Cybil War** Betsy Byars

☐ FM 40529-2 **Amy and Laura** Marilyn Sachs

☐ FM 40950-6 **The Girl with the Silver Eyes** Willo Davis Roberts

☐ FM 40755-4 **Ghosts Beneath Our Feet** Betty Ren Wright

☐ FM 40605-1 **Help! I'm a Prisoner in the Library** Eth Clifford

☐ FM 40724-4 **Katie's Baby-sitting Job** Martha Tolles

☐ FM 40607-8 **Secrets in the Attic** Carol Beach York

☐ FM 40534-9 **This Can't Be Happening at Macdonald Hall!**
              Gordon Korman

☐ FM 40687-6 **Just Tell Me When We're Dead!** Eth Clifford